This book
belongs to

............................

To Sam

FREDERICK WARNE

Published by the Penguin Group
Penguin Books Ltd, 80 Strand, London WC2R oRL, England
Penguin Young Readers Group, 345 Hudson Street,
New York, New York 10014, U.S.A.
Penguin Books Australia Ltd, 250 Camberwell Road, Camberwell,
Victoria 3124, Australia
Canada, India, New Zealand, South Africa

1 3 5 7 9 10 8 6 4 2

ISBN-13: 978 07232 5797 4
ISBN-10: 0 7232 5797 3

Printed in Great Britain

Zinnia's
Magical
Adventure

by Pippa Le Quesne

Welcome to the Flower Fairy Garden!

Where are the fairies?
Where can we find them?
We've seen the fairy-rings
They leave behind them!

Is it a secret
No one is telling?
Why, in your garden
Surely they're dwelling!

No need for journeying,
Seeking afar:
Where there are flowers,
There fairies are!

# Contents

Chapter One
## Babysitting                                    I

Chapter Two
## High Up!                                       II

Chapter Three
## Time to Explore                                21

Chapter Four
## New Friends                                    35

Chapter Five
## Naughty Elves                                  49

Chapter Six
## Bedtime Stories                                65

# Chapter One
## Babysitting

'Yes, Your Majesty, I agree. Daisy does make quite the best fairy nectar in the garden,' Zinnia said, lifting her bluebell cup and pretending to take a dainty sip.

Daisy giggled as she got to her feet, gathering the petals of her skirt in either hand. 'Show me how you curtsey again,' she said, putting out a leg in front of her and wobbling as she tried to bob down without losing her balance.

'Watch out!' Double Daisy shouted. 'Or you'll land in the crab-apple jelly – and imagine what the Queen of the Meadow would think of that!'

The two young Flower Fairies burst out laughing.

Zinnia smiled to herself. Her little cousins were very sweet and she loved spending time with them but it had been a long morning since Daisy had come up with the idea of a make-believe royal tea party. Zinnia had made special daisy-chain garlands for each of them and patiently tried to teach them how they should bow and curtsey in front

of a queen. Double Daisy would lean so far
forwards that the red petals from his bonnet
kept flopping in his eyes, causing him to
topple over, and he and his sister to fall about
laughing. And of course no matter how many
times he did it, the funnier the two of them
found it.

It had been very funny at first and
Zinnia had been happy to have imaginary
conversations with their regal guest, but now
she was getting a bit bored of the game and
longed to stretch her legs.

She couldn't help wondering what Beechnut and Hazelnut were up to. These cheeky fairies were always bursting with energy and up for a game of tag. The trouble was that they lived in the lane outside the garden boundaries. And Daisy and Double Daisy were too little to stray far from their flowers and too young to be left on their own.

Now they were concentrating hard on carrying bark plates piled high with imaginary food, supposedly presenting them to their guest. They were also arguing about whether the Queen of the Meadow would have arrived in a chariot pulled by dragonflies or if she would fly in from the marshes on the back of a bird.

Zinnia sighed. It had been ages since she had been out of the garden and it suddenly struck her that she must have been missing out on all sorts of excitement. Beechnut and

Hazelnut got to see everything from their vantage point in the trees and they were always full of interesting stories – for a start, lots of different humans used the lane to go about their daily business. Zinnia often spent time imagining what it would be like to live somewhere less predictable than the garden.

'You're daydreaming again!' a voice from above interrupted her thoughts.

Zinnia looked up. A Flower Fairy with rosy cheeks and pretty pink wings was sitting on the bough of the apple tree, swinging her legs.

'Apple Blossom!'

Zinnia was very pleased to see her friend. She was always cheerful and never got tired of playing with the younger

Flower Fairies.

'I was just thinking it might be nice to see what's going on in the lane this afternoon…' Zinnia paused. She suddenly had an idea. 'Um, but of course I'm looking after my cousins,' she went on, 'and I would ask Sweet Pea, but she's busy teaching the baby fairies to climb…'

'I'd love to look after Daisy and Double Daisy,' Apple Blossom interrupted. 'Off you go and have an adventure!' She began nimbly swinging from branch to branch until she was perched on the tip of the one nearest to the ground.

'Oh, you're brilliant!' Zinnia beamed as Apple Blossom flew down and landed on the grass.

The Tree Fairy gathered up Daisy in an enormous hug and then swung Double Daisy round and round by his arms.

'What are you up to, my lovelies?'

'We're having tea with the Queen of the Meadow, of course,' the two Daisies chorused.

'Well, good afternoon, Your Highness, what an honour,' Apple Blossom said, winking at Zinnia and curtseying very low to the space between the two young Flower Fairies.

Zinnia waved goodbye and blew a kiss to her cousins. They would have a great time with Apple Blossom and she'd be back long before their bedtime. As she headed for the wall at the bottom of the garden there was a definite spring to her step and she felt a sudden surge of excitement. She had the whole afternoon to herself and who knew what lay ahead of her?

# Chapter Two
## High Up!

'Horse Chestnut! Where are you?' Zinnia
called, parting the large green leaves of his
tree to peer up among the higher branches.
She had made light work of the garden
wall, which was old stone and had plenty
of footholds, and, after a quick look up and
down the lane to check it was safe, she had
flown straight for her friend's tree.

'Horse Chestnut, are you there?'

Zinnia ran lightly along the length of the branch until she was right inside the canopy of leaves, where she leant against the trunk of the tree to catch her breath. She tucked a loose strand of hair behind her ear and straightened the daisy garland on her head, expecting Horse Chestnut's mischievous face to appear at any moment.

*Mind you*, she thought, *it would be more like him to come whizzing out of nowhere and surprise me!*

Horse Chestnut always dressed entirely in green and brown, including his green spiky helmet, so he was quite difficult to spot and an expert at sudden appearances.

'Today I will be ready for him,' Zinnia said resolutely, thinking aloud. She listened intently for any sign of movement but could only hear the distant song of a blackbird and the leaves of the tree stirring gently in the breeze.

After a few moments without any sign of Horse Chestnut, Zinnia began to relax.

She watched a field mouse dart across the dusty lane and scurry into a hedgerow and wondered if Horse Chestnut had gone to visit Beechnut. She would go and look for both of them in a minute, she decided, but for now she was enjoying her view of the world from above. Being high up made her aware that she was out in a much larger open space than usual, and compared to the garden with

its familiar beds and borders, it seemed to brim with possibilities.

At that moment, Zinnia's thoughts were interrupted by the sound of excited chatter followed by a loud laugh. It seemed to be coming from further up the lane. And if she wasn't mistaken, it was the sound of human children heading towards her!

Taking care to be as quiet as she could, Zinnia crept along the branch to get a better view. Luckily there was a particularly large horse chestnut leaf for her to hide behind, and flattening her wings against her back she made sure that none of the bright pink petals of her skirt were poking out.

You see, Flower Fairies can see humans and they know all about them. They are even allowed to help humans, but on no account are they ever to let humans catch sight of them. When Zinnia had officially been given her flower and become a proper Flower Fairy, wise Wild Rose had explained to her that generally humans were very friendly. However, they were also curious beings – especially children – and if they knew that there really were fairies living in their world and even in their own gardens they would never leave them alone and it would be impossible for Flower Fairyland to continue its peaceful existence.

Zinnia took a deep breath and bravely popped her head out from behind the leaf. She had seen the humans that lived in the house at the top of the garden on numerous occasions, but the insects would feel the vibrations in the grass first and always give the fairies ample warning. This time Zinnia was unprepared and she was alone.

The children were nearly below the tree now. A boy and a girl with dark hair and very similar features were hurrying along at quite a pace and a smaller girl with flushed red cheeks was struggling to keep up with them.

'Come on, Emily, you're such a slow coach!' the boy called to her.

'Shut up, Tom,' she replied, puffing. 'If it wasn't for me you'd still be complaining about how boring playing in the garden is.'

'And she was the last one to climb over the gate,' his twin sister reminded him. 'Anyway, because it was Emily's idea to explore the marsh she should lead the way.'

'Who made you expedition organizer, Charlotte?' Tom said, but Zinnia could see that he had a grin on his face and he'd slowed down so that his younger sister could catch up.

'Will there be quicksand? Who do you think we'll meet on the marsh? Do wild animals live there?' Emily chirruped away – too busy asking questions to wait for the answers.

Zinnia watched them disappearing down the lane, not moving a muscle for several moments. The Flower Fairy wasn't fixed to the spot because she was afraid they'd catch sight of her – they had been so absorbed in their conversation that they hadn't even looked up once – but because she'd had a brainwave. She'd never been to the marsh and she'd certainly never met any of the Wild Flower Fairies that lived there. Their very name suggested that they must be far more exotic than any of the fairies Zinnia knew. That was it!

Forget playing tag in the lane, she was off for a real adventure.

'Show me the way!' she called boldly after the retreating figures, knowing that her voice was too tiny for them to hear at a distance. With that, she took an joyous leap into the air and beat her wings as fast as she could in order to follow the children.

'You're it!'

Charlotte shrieked with glee as she tagged her brother. She turned on her heel, her shoes squelching along the boggy path as she ran.

'Mum's going to kill us!' Emily giggled as she dived into the long rush-grass, just managing to escape Tom's grasp.

The marsh was like nowhere Zinnia had ever been before.

The children had climbed over a stile that led

directly from the lane on to the marsh and she had done her best to keep up with them as they splashed along the waterlogged path that cut across it. They whooped and called to one another, flitting in and out of the tall grasses. To the Flower Fairy, the long grass seemed like a forest compared to the short spiky grass that neatly bordered the flower bed where she lived.

When finally the children had taken a break from their game to catch their breath, Zinnia landed on a grass with dense and cottony heads. It provided her with a comfortable resting place. The marshland seemed to stretch as far as she could see in every direction – a sea of grass that met the horizon, the muted green unbroken by any of the bright flowers or blossom trees that she was used to.

In comparison, the fuchsia pink of her skirt looked even more dazzling than usual and so she had to be doubly careful not to let the children spot her.

At first Zinnia had flown behind them at a safe distance, but soon she became bolder and it wasn't long before she was so close that if they'd turned their heads she wouldn't have more than a split second to hide. And then it became a game of dare – weaving in and out of the grasses after the

children, or darting on to the path and flying
right behind them before plunging back
amidst the stalks at the last moment.

*Phew!* she thought to herself as she sank back into the fluffy cushions. *Apple Blossom and the Daisies will never believe how far I've flown today.* She smiled to herself, imagining their surprise.

Garden Flower Fairies don't fly long distances – they walk as much as they can and tend to take to the air to get up into the trees or just for fun. If they have further to go they hitch a lift with a friendly bird or dragonfly. Zinnia was just picturing her friends' faces as she told them all about the children and following them to the marsh, when a flash of purple caught her eye. She felt a rush of adrenalin. Could it be one of the Wild Flower Fairies that she'd come to meet? Tingling with anticipation she launched herself into the air to find out.

When she landed she headed in the
direction she thought the fairy had taken.
And sure enough – just beyond the path,
behind a clump of rush-grass – sat not just
one Flower Fairy but three!

The fairy that Zinnia had seen sat with her
knees pulled up to her chin, a torn green
smock all but covering her purple petal-
dress and her long brown hair pulled back in

two messy plaits. She had beautiful purple and white wings, but Zinnia was shocked to see how dusty they looked – she had never come across a Flower Fairy that seemed to care less about her appearance! In front of her were two boy fairies – both with pointed ears, plain white wings and, Zinnia noticed, clothes the colour of the surrounding grasses. In fact one of them had tufty blond hair like the flower head that she'd sat on and the other wore a grass girdle around his tunic that was hemmed with small brown seeds.

'Er, hello,' she ventured, feeling quite nervous as she stepped out into the clearing.

'Wow, look at you!' the female Flower Fairy burst out, jumping to her feet. 'I've never seen such magnificent wings.'

'They're the same as the painted lady butterflies,' Zinnia said timidly. 'And my skirt is from my flower – Zinnia,' she added, quite taken aback by the confident fairy who was walking slowly round her, openly admiring her clothes.

'I'm Mallow, but most people call me Rags-and-Tatters on account of the state of me!' Mallow laughed warmly and Zinnia couldn't help but like her immediately.

'And I'm Cotton-Grass and this is my brother Rush-Grass,' the blond boy fairy said, pointing to his companion, whose cheeky face broke into a broad grin.

'Come and join us – we've been spying on some newcomers,' said Mallow, cocking her head in the direction of

the sound of the children's chatter. She sat
down and patted the ground next to her.
'And you're certainly not from around here,
looking as neat as a new pin!'

'I'm from the garden,' Zinnia explained.
'Quite a long way from here, actually,' she
went on, no longer feeling shy.

'Oh, the garden,' Rush-Grass said. 'Heard
all about it, but never been myself.'

'I've seen it once.' Mallow nodded wisely. 'Peeked over the wall on my travels. I sell my seeds as fairy cheeses at the market. Fairy housewives and elves can't get enough of them!' she explained, picking up from beside her what looked to Zinnia like a miniature pumpkin.

'That garden's very cosy-looking', said Cotton-Grass.

'Sounds a bit tame, if you ask me,' piped up Rush-Grass – but not unkindly.

Zinnia wasn't sure if she liked her home being called cosy or tame. It was very ordered and life was comfortable there, but she didn't want the marsh dwellers to think she was boring.

'Oh, but there's always plenty going on. And um, I don't really spend much time there – I'm always off exploring,' she boasted uncertainly.

'Well, you should come and see the sights with us. Never a dull moment on the marsh. Every day's an adventure!' Cotton-Grass said enthusiastically, 'and the best part is that we never know where we'll be at nightfall.'

'What do you mean?' Zinnia asked, enthralled.

'Sleep where we end up – make do with whatever pillow we can find, of course!' Rush-Grass exclaimed, jumping to his feet and stretching his arms out wide.

'You should try it. Nothing beats sleeping out – with nothing between you and the stars. How about tonight?' Cotton-Grass offered.

Zinnia gulped. The thought of darkness drawing in without the comfort of her familiar flower or a moss blanket to pull over her wasn't very appealing – even if it was an adventure … But on the other hand, she couldn't let her new friends think she was any less courageous than them. No – she would show them what a Garden Flower Fairy was made of!

## Chapter Four
## New Friends

Just then there was a low whistle from a
nearby clump of grass.

'Hey, Cotton, Rush – come here, I think
you're needed,' whispered Mallow, who had
wandered off to keep an eye on the children.

Zinnia had been vaguely aware of the
absence of laughter and the tone of the
children's voices changing. And now, as
she peeked over Mallow's shoulder,
it was obvious that they
were no longer enjoying
themselves.

They were quite a different sight from the three children who had been in high spirits earlier that afternoon. Aside from the messy state of their clothes, they looked tired and decidedly miserable.

'I'm starving,' Tom complained loudly, kicking at a muddy puddle with the toe of his shoe.

'There's no use in saying that over and over again,' said Charlotte. 'You know we've missed tea and we'll be lucky if Mum doesn't send us to bed without anything to eat.'

'And we still haven't found my shoe,'
Emily wailed. She was in particularly bad
shape – her plump little legs and feet were
caked in mud and her skirt was covered in
grass stains. Zinnia thought she looked
quite comical and it reminded her of her
Daisy cousins, which in turn made her feel
quite homesick.

'Seeing as you don't even know when it
came off, we're never going to find it,'
Tom said grumpily. 'And I don't
know about you – but I've
no idea what direction we
came from.'

Charlotte, who was
frantically searching
through the grass,
looked up. 'We just
need to find the path
and then even if we go

in the wrong direction at least we'll know the other way will take us back to the lane,' she said, looking less sure than she sounded.

'That's our job,' Rush-Grass whispered to Zinnia. 'We help whoever's got lost on the marsh to find their way home.'

'How do you do that without them seeing you though?' Zinnia asked.

'A little bit of fairy dust and a bit more

speed,' chortled Cotton-Grass, who was unfolding a large dock leaf that he had been carrying as a knapsack.

'People generally follow bright lights – even if it isn't dark – it makes them feel hopeful.' Rush-Grass beamed at Zinnia. 'So we just catch their eye with some fairy dust, make some noise and then fly to the path as fast as we can.' He took a handful of the fine powder.

'Perhaps you should go back with them,' Mallow suggested. 'It's time that I got myself ready for market tomorrow, so I'd better be off.'

Zinnia was about to gratefully agree when she remembered their conversation about the garden and how she'd boasted about being adventurous. Although she wasn't sure she knew her way home she felt confident that if she flew above the grass she'd get her bearings quickly enough. 'Oh, don't worry about me,' she said cheerily. 'I've still got some exploring to do.'

'Travel well, then,' Cotton said, opening his wings.

'Farewell, ladies,' said his brother. As he took off he blew the fairy dust into the air. 'Light up!' he commanded.

Zinnia watched the tiny particles glow to life and dance away on the breeze. 'Goodbye!' she called as the Grass Fairies followed.

'Well,' said Mallow, turning to the Garden Fairy and taking her hands, 'it's been lovely to meet you and I hope it's not the last time.'

She turned to go and then as an afterthought held out a fat mallow seed.

Zinnia took it gratefully and waved as her friend disappeared through the tall grass. 'Maybe see you later?' she called after her, as it suddenly struck her that she was completely alone again.

'I'll eat the cheese and then I'll be on my way,' Zinnia said, thinking aloud into the silence. It wasn't until she sat down that she realized how tired she was – all the excitement had kept her exhaustion at bay but now her wings positively ached. 'If only I'd brought some fairy dust with me.'

Flower Fairies cannot cast spells but

ground-up pollen from each of their flowers gives them a little magic of their own. Walking all the way home seemed like an impossible task to Zinnia but if she had some of her fairy dust she could have summoned the butterflies to accompany her.

*Perhaps I am going to have to sleep here tonight*, she thought, as she took a bite of the cheese. The mallow seed was delicious and instantly comforting and somehow helped her forget about her butterfly friends: some of Mallow's magic. Zinnia smiled as her spirits lifted further and she reminded herself that plenty of Wild Flower Fairies slept out on the marsh, so it couldn't be that frightening.

She was just thinking that Cotton-Grass and Rush-Grass might be back before too long when she was startled by a rustling in the grass behind her. She looked around but there was no one.

There it was again – more rustling, but this time to the left of her and it was followed by a stifled giggle.

'Rush? Cotton? Is that you?'

But there was no answer, just more rustling.

'Mallow?' Zinnia called optimistically, hoping that her friend had finished her work quickly and come back to find her.

The Garden Fairy got to her feet and shivered. The heat had gone out of the

afternoon sun and for the first time she
noticed how much colder it was without the
shelter of the garden wall.

*I may as well start heading home*, she thought,
*even if I don't find the path, at least moving will
warm me up.*

Hearing another giggle, Zinnia hurried
to pick up the remainder of the mallow seed.
But she was too late – the grasses parted and
two creatures dressed entirely in dark green
rushed out at her.

'Fairy cheese and a pretty little
fairy to go with it!' said
one gleefully and
the other snatched
the seed from her
hands, causing
her to lose her
balance.

Zinnia looked up at the sly eyes staring back
at her; then she looked at the long pointed
ears and the hoods covering messy hair.
And finally she noticed not only the muddy,
unwashed feet but, more importantly, the
pointed wings on the back of the creatures.

'You're elves!' Zinnia gasped and before
she could stop herself, she burst into tears.

## Chapter Five
# Naughty Elves

'Crybaby! Crybaby!' chanted the elves, dancing round Zinnia in delight.

At first they had been stunned into silence by the Garden Fairy's outburst, but now that she had dried her eyes and was looking cross rather than sad, they had set about poking fun at her.

After shedding a few tears, Zinnia felt a lot better and now the elves were infuriating her. Their energy seemed to be limitless and no matter how many times she tried to dodge past one of them, the other would be there, barring her way. 'Give me back my cheese and let me go!' she exclaimed, trying to grab the mallow seed from the nearest elf as he blocked her path.

But he threw it over her head to his companion, giggling almost uncontrollably.

'Shan't give you the cheese – that's ours
for the eating,' said the other elf, taking an
enormous bite and all but finishing it off.
'But you're free to go whenever you want,
isn't she?' He winked at his friend and threw
him back the last of the mallow seed.

'Although that's not to say we won't follow
you, pretty one,' mocked his companion,
cramming what was left into his mouth.

'Elves – you're trespassing!' boomed a voice that stopped all three of them in their tracks, and the next moment into the clearing walked the most resplendent Flower Fairy Zinnia had ever seen. He was older than her with a distinguished air about him but he had a youthful, handsome face. Apart from his leaf-green mantle and slippers, he was clothed from head to toe in shimmering gold and on his head he wore a crown of bright yellow flower stamens.

'Kingcup!' breathed Zinnia, trembling a little as she curtseyed.

When she looked up she saw that the king was smiling at her tenderly and although this was the first time she had met him, she felt instantly at ease.

As for the elves, they were a pathetic sight – cowering before the regal Flower Fairy – unrecognizable as the two creatures that had been taunting Zinnia just moments before.

'You are trespassing on Flower Fairy territory.' Kingcup turned to them. 'And for stealing from one of my kind you are banished from the marsh – now be gone!'

The elves scrambled to their feet. 'Yes, Your Majesty,' and 'many apologies, Your Majesty,' they mumbled as they fell over one another to escape from the clearing first.

When they had gone, the king turned back to Zinnia with a twinkle in his eye. 'Well, I think they were suitably told off, don't you? They don't really mean any harm; they just can't resist fairy cheese.' He chuckled and then added, 'or teasing!'

Zinnia breathed a sigh of relief. 'Thank you so much for rescuing me,' she said gratefully. 'I realized fairly soon that they weren't dangerous – but they were maddening and they wouldn't let me go.'

'Presumably you mean home?' Kingcup

said, taking Zinnia by the hand and leading
her out of the clearing. Soon they had found
the path, and as they walked he asked her,
'What are you doing so far from the garden
so late in the day?'

Zinnia began relaying the events of the afternoon, feeling a little foolish when it came to the part about showing off to the Wild Flower Fairies, but the king just smiled as if it was a mistake he could have easily made himself.

'Well,' said Kingcup when she had finished, 'I'm assuming that you'd like to go back to the garden tonight?' He waited for Zinnia to nod in response. 'Then you're in luck. A dear friend of mine that is visiting will be heading back your way and I'm sure

she'd be more than glad to take you.'

They'd left the path now and were picking their way across much wetter ground. Soon there were small pools of water and it was not long before it was obvious to Zinnia that they had reached Kingcup's realm. Growing out of the pools were clusters of marsh marigolds with their kidney-shaped leaves and shiny golden flowers like giant buttercups. And sitting among them was a willowy Flower Fairy with long blonde hair, delicate shell-pink wings and a tiara of rose stamens.

'Wild Rose!' Zinnia cried out happily.

'So, I see your stroll was rather eventful,' Wild Rose remarked to Kingcup as she fluttered over to join them. She kissed the top of Zinnia's head and murmured, 'Sweet Garden Fairy – what are you doing here?'

'She's been having a grand adventure on the marsh,' the king replied in good humour. 'And I'm sure she'll tell you all about it on your way home.'

'Oh yes, of course.' Wild Rose nodded wisely. Then glancing at the weary Garden Fairy, she said, 'I think we'll summon a moorhen and see if we can catch a ride home.'

Zinnia was very pleased to hear that they wouldn't be making the journey on foot as ever since she had been in the comforting presence of Wild Rose, waves of tiredness had begun to wash over her. She would have gladly slept in precisely the spot she was standing.

Once Kingcup had clapped his hands, they didn't have to wait for more than a few moments before a friendly looking bird with black glossy feathers and a vivid red and yellow beak landed in the water beside them. Without further ado, the king bade them farewell. 'Goodbye, Rose, see you soon,' he said, kissing her on both cheeks.

Zinnia watched Wild Rose mount the moorhen and sit elegantly with her legs and skirt to one side. Then she clambered up in front of her and wrapped her arms around the bird's neck in preparation for take-off. 'It was an honour to meet you, Your Majesty,' she called to Kingcup. 'Sorry you had to come and save me.'

'It was a pleasure – and anyway, I didn't really save you. You were being very brave and the elves would have tired of their game soon enough. Now off you go!'

\* \* \*

'You know, I do enjoy living in the hedgerow and meeting all the Flower Fairies that pass by or come to visit me to be named. And I quite understand the lure of the unknown,' said Wild Rose gently, 'but you're very lucky to have a flower that resides out of harm's way. You've always a wonderful variety of company – so many different fairies to play with but all with familiar faces – as well as your own special butterfly friends.'

Zinnia turned to say something in reply, but Wild Rose just raised a finger to her lips. 'Look – here's the lane. We'll be there soon.'

As they'd soared above the marsh, Zinnia had gazed down at the vast exposed area below and she'd had a sense of just how small she was in comparison. Even with Wild Rose's arms encircling her waist she'd suddenly felt quite lost and as she listened to the words of the older Flower Fairy she longed to be back in the garden. And there, far below them, but now in sight, was the garden. Zinnia's heart leapt at the sight of it and, with every ounce of her being, she willed the moorhen to fly faster.

# Chapter Six
## Bedtime Stories

'I didn't meet the Queen of the Meadow but I did meet Kingcup!'

Zinnia was sitting on the edge of the moss blanket under which Daisy and Double Daisy were snuggled, telling her two little cousins all about her adventure.

There had been great excitement when she had arrived on the back of the moorhen. It wasn't often that Wild Rose visited the garden but she had a reputation as being the kindest and wisest of the Flower Fairies and was greatly loved by all that knew her. Zinnia had proudly introduced Wild Rose to Daisy and Double Daisy – who lost no time in informing her all about their royal tea party and showing her their very best curtsey and bow, which Apple Blossom had been helping them perfect.

'Can you stay until bedtime?' Double
Daisy had begged, after insisting that she
come and see the corner of the garden that
he and Daisy lived in, where their star-like
flowers were still lifting their faces to catch
the last rays of sunshine.

'I've had a very long day out on the moor,'
replied Wild Rose, 'and it's time I was getting
home, but I promise to come back for one
of your splendid tea parties. Besides, I have
a feeling that someone has a particularly
interesting bedtime story to tell you tonight,'

she added, looking directly at Zinnia.

When they had said their goodbyes and
the Daisies had stopped jumping around
at the thought of entertaining Wild Rose,
Zinnia finally managed to settle them down
for the night. The two little Flower Fairies
sat upright in their bed, their blanket pulled
up to their chins and listened with shining
eyes as she told them all about following the
children to the marsh and how she had met
Cotton-Grass, Rush-Grass and Mallow.
They asked her to repeat the bit about the
elves three times before she could get to the
part where Kingcup rescued her and took her
to find Wild Rose.

'What was the best bit of the day?' Daisy asked, rubbing her eyes sleepily.

'Coming home to you two,' Zinnia said without hesitation, leaning over to kiss them both goodnight.

As the sun sank behind the garden wall and the last of the daisies closed its petals for the night, Zinnia sighed happily to herself. How could she ever get bored of the sight of her cousins sinking peacefully into sleep? She stood up and yawned. She couldn't imagine wanting to go off on an adventure for quite some time now but the next time she did, it would be with the knowledge that the only place that she belonged at the end of the day was safely tucked up in her cosy corner of the garden.

Visit our Flower Fairies website at:

# www.flowerfairies.com

There are lots of fun Flower Fairy games and
activities for you to play, plus you can find out more
about all your favourite fairy friends!

# More tales from these Flower Fairies coming soon!

Almond Blossom

Candytuft

Buttercup

Strawberry